my World® of Wicked Pirates

Peg Leg Meg

Meg gave up being a pirate two years ago and now lives the life of a landlubber with her husband, John. She has a gypsy caravan where she writes about the secrets of the sea and a dog whom she is training to look for treasure, but so far he has only found bones. She tries to follow the pirates' code but finds it very difficult (especially rule no.6).

Lucy Blackheart

Lucy lives in an enchanting faraway land where she paints pictures about her favourite things. She has often imagined having exciting adventures and discovering treasure islands and meeting mermaids. However, she would much rather stay at home painting about the life of a pirate than suffer the hardships of being a real one herself.

We dedicate this book to Simona – a real treasure!

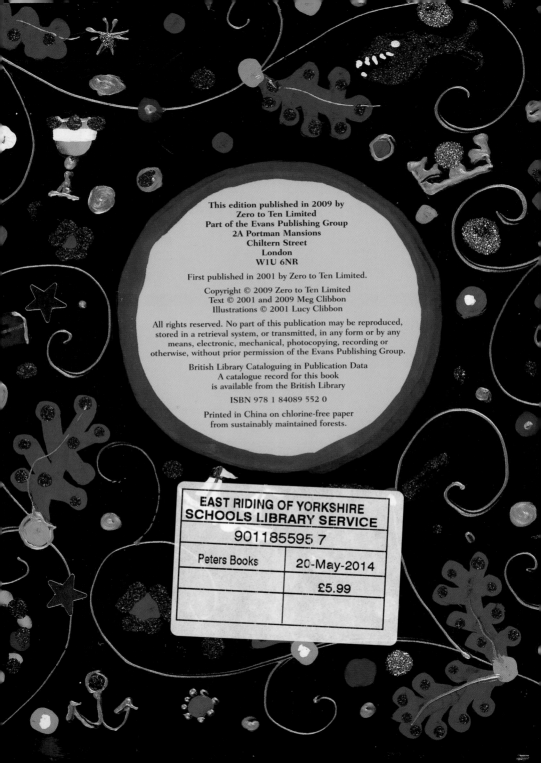

This edition published in 2009 by
Zero to Ten Limited
Part of the Evans Publishing Group
2A Portman Mansions
Chiltern Street
London
W1U 6NR

First published in 2001 by Zero to Ten Limited.

Copyright © 2009 Zero to Ten Limited
Text © 2001 and 2009 Meg Clibbon
Illustrations © 2001 Lucy Clibbon

British Library Cataloguing in Publication Data
A catalogue record for this book
is available from the British Library

ISBN 978 1 84089 552 0

Printed in China on chlorine-free paper
from sustainably maintained forests.

EAST RIDING
OF YORKSHIRE COUNCIL
Schools Library Service

PROJECT
June 2014

Contents

What is a pirate?

aaargh!

Definition:
a robber who attacks
ships at sea.

What do pirates look like?

There are some pirates who are big and strong and bold.

There are some pirates who are tall and thin and cunning.

Pirates can come in many different shapes and sizes but...
all pirates are very, very wicked.

Becoming a pirate

You can become a pirate by running away from home with all your things tied up in a spotted hanky. You have to walk to the nearest port and become a cabin boy or girl on a pirate ship. Then you have to learn how to be very, very wicked. This takes a long time and gets a bit boring after a while, so most people prefer to stay at home and watch a bit of television with something delicious to eat!

The pirate code

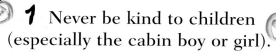

1 Never be kind to children (especially the cabin boy or girl).

2 Never be kind to mermaids.

3 Never be kind to anyone.

4 Always look fierce.

5 Always carry a cutlass.

6 Always obey the captain.

The pirate motto:

Rob or rot!

What do pirates wear?

Hat

Spotted hanky

Earrings

Baggy shirt

This hand is sometimes missing.

Belt

Baggy trousers

Sea boots

This leg is sometimes missing.

Equipment and accessories

In order to be a pirate you will need some of the following equipment and accessories...

Spotted hanky

Eye patch

Earrings

Spade

Cutlass

Dagger

Wooden leg
or hook

Scrubbing
brush

Parrot

Three-cornered hat
with gold braid

Stick on Tattoos

Bottle of grog

Where do pirates work?

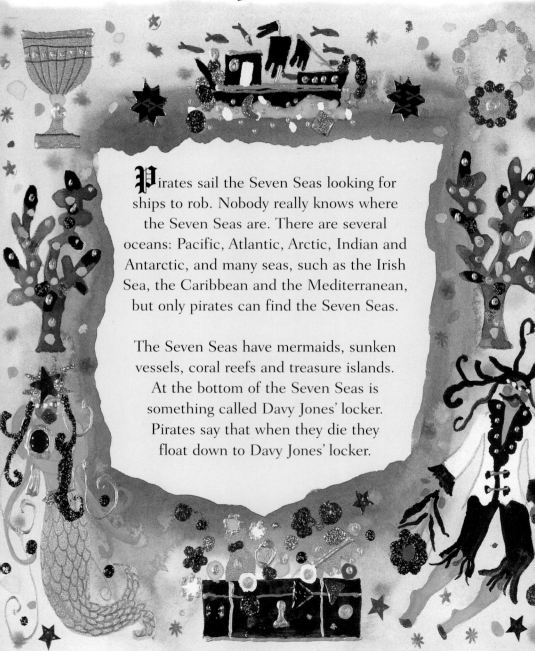

Pirates sail the Seven Seas looking for ships to rob. Nobody really knows where the Seven Seas are. There are several oceans: Pacific, Atlantic, Arctic, Indian and Antarctic, and many seas, such as the Irish Sea, the Caribbean and the Mediterranean, but only pirates can find the Seven Seas.

The Seven Seas have mermaids, sunken vessels, coral reefs and treasure islands. At the bottom of the Seven Seas is something called Davy Jones' locker. Pirates say that when they die they float down to Davy Jones' locker.

The Jolly Roger

You can always recognise a pirate ship because it will be flying the pirate flag called the **'Jolly Roger'**. It is a black flag with a white skull and crossed thigh bones on it, sometimes known as the skull and crossbones. When you see this flag you should be very, very frightened!

The ship and her captain

Imagine you are the captain of a real pirate ship. Think of a really wicked name for the ship and then draw a picture of what you'd like her to look like.

'Who's a pretty boy then?'

Black Revenge

The only friends that pirates really have are parrots, because they sit on their shoulders and say funny things like, **'Who's a pretty boy then?'**.

Food and drink

They eat lots of fish.

Pirates are at sea for most of the time so they don't get much fresh food. They do not eat enough vitamins so they have spots and scurvy. Scurvy is a nasty disease you get when you don't eat the right sort of food.

They also drink lots of rum, or grog, which they like better than the water kept in barrels on deck.

They eat lots of ship's biscuits, which are very maggoty.

Pirate songs

When pirates have been drinking, they like nothing better than to sing a jolly pirate song.
Here are two of their favourites:

Fifteen men on a dead man's chest
Yo ho ho and a bottle of rum
Drink and the devil had
done for the rest
Yo ho ho and a bottle of rum

What shall we do with
the drunken pirate?
What shall we do with
the drunken pirate?
What shall we do with
the drunken pirate,
early in the morning?

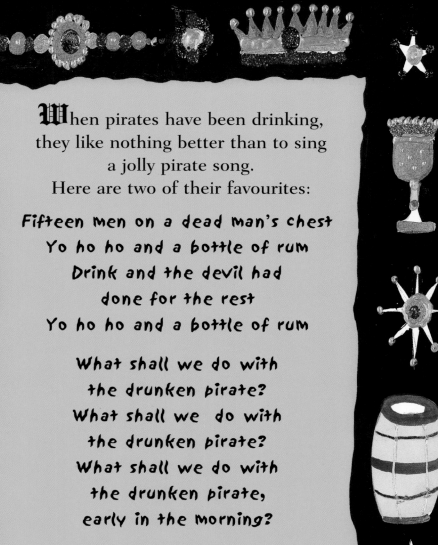

Pirates behaving badly

When pirates disobey the pirate captain they can be cruelly punished in a number of ways…

Scrubbing the deck

(This is the worst punishment.) They have to pull up a bucket of salty water from the sea, get down on hands and knees with a scrubbing brush and scrub the entire deck with a constant circular motion until it is clean. Oh dear!

Flogging

The captain ties them to the mast and hits them with a nasty whip with long strands, called a cat o' nine tails, until they are very sorry. Then he throws salt water onto their wounds. Oh dear! Oh dear!

Walking the plank

When pirates capture other ships they sometimes make their captives walk the plank. They tie a plank to the deck so that it sticks out over the sea. Then they make their victims walk to the end so that they fall in –

SPLASH !

Wanted!

Wanted
Black Hearted Bill
For evil deeds on the High Seas
Description: Black greasy hair, dirty teeth,
snarling lips, scar on chin, black moustache.

Beware!
Do not approach this pirate.

Pirate phrases

Yo ho ho, the frisky plank...

Ready about skipper.

Pieces of eight...

All hands on deck.

Avast there!

Splice the mainbrace.

Land ahoy!

Man overboard!

Look astern, matey.

Aye, aye, cap'n!

Stand by to go about.

Shiver me timbers!

Famous pirates

Captain Hook

Captain Hook is the pirate in J.M. Barrie's book, *Peter Pan*. He had a hook because Peter Pan chopped off his hand with a sword during a fight.

A passing crocodile had eaten the hand and he chased after Captain Hook to try to eat the rest of him. Fortunately he had also swallowed an alarm clock, so Captain Hook always knew when the crocodile was coming.

Long John Silver

Long John Silver is the pirate in *Treasure Island* by R.L. Stevenson. He pretended to be an honest man on board a ship called the *Hispaniola*, which was searching for treasure, but really he was the head of a pirate gang who were after the treasure for themselves. Long John Silver had a wooden leg and a parrot who screeched,

"pieces of eight... pieces of eight".

Pirate things to do

Message in a bottle

Imagine that you have been captured by pirates and then marooned on a deserted island. You need to be rescued! Write a message which can be sealed up in a bottle and thrown into the sea.

Wanted Poster

Make your own **Wanted** poster by dressing up your best friend as a pirate and drawing a picture of them. Try inventing your own 'olde worlde' style of writing for the words on the poster.

Pirates' treasure map

To help pirates find treasure they always have a map, which is usually very, very old. It is dipped in tea and torn around the edges, then rolled up and fastened with ribbon. Can you make your own treasure map?

Pirate grog

𝕿his is a drink which pirates make to keep them warm on deck. It also has plenty of vitamin C in it, which stops them from getting scurvy.

For each pirate you need:

1 lemon
1 tablespoon of brown sugar
1 pinch of powdered ginger
1 jug of hot water

Directions

1 Cut the lemon in half and squeeze out the juice.
2 Put juice in jug and add sugar and ginger.
3 Add hot water and stir well.

Pirate Billy Sails Away

the story of a runaway pirate

Once, there was a boy called Billy, who lived with his mother, father and little sister in a house beside the sea. He loved reading and his favourite book was all about pirates. At night he dreamt about sailing the Seven Seas to look for coral islands with buried treasure. His duvet cover had pictures of cutlasses, pirate ships and the Jolly Roger on it.

One morning, things started badly for him. His mother called, "Billy, have you made your bed and cleaned your teeth? Oh – and I wish you wouldn't wear your boots in the house."

His father called, "Billy, come and help me clean the car, will you? Oh – and is it you that's been digging for buried treasure in my vegetable patch?"

His little sister just cried and pulled his hair.

Billy thought, "Pirates don't clean their teeth and make their beds. No one tells them to take off their sea boots. And they don't have cars to clean or annoying little sisters. I'm going to run away and become a pirate."

So he did.

It just so happened that a pirate ship was docked at the quayside and the gangplank was down. A fierce-looking pirate was standing guard. Billy said, "I've run away to be a pirate."

The pirate snarled, "Can yer cook?"

"Yes, sir," said Billy.

"Can yer scrub decks?"

"Yes, sir," said Billy.

"Can yer run errands?"

"Yes, sir," said Billy.

"Can yer swim?"

"No, sir!" said Billy.

"Oh dear, oh dearie me," chuckled the pirate to himself. "Whatever. You'd better come and meet the captain."

The captain was huge and ugly and ferocious. He had dirty black curly hair and a dirty black curly beard with bits of food stuck in it.

The captain made Billy do all the worst jobs on the ship. He had to scrub the deck with cold seawater, climb up the rigging to the crow's nest in icy gales and, worst of all, take the parrot for a walk. It sat on his shoulder and pecked him and squawked, "Pretty Polly".

All day long Billy ran up and down between decks, fetching and carrying things for the captain and the other pirates. Were they grateful? No way! It was, "Shiver me timbers, this," and "Shiver me timbers, that," or "Billy, hoist the Jolly Roger and be quick about it, or it's the frisky plank for you," or "Splice the mainbrace and look alive, matey."

Billy didn't know what they were talking about most of the time. Well, would you? At the end of each day, all Billy had to eat were dry ship's biscuits (complete with maggots), and all he had to drink was dirty water from a barrel on deck. The pirates drank grog and sang very noisy songs. He slept in a hammock down at the bottom of the ship with all the other smelly, noisy pirates and several rats. There were no portholes and NO ensuite bathrooms.

After a week on the ship, Billy still hadn't seen any coral islands and he certainly hadn't found any treasure. He was hungry, tired and sick of big waves and noisy pirates. At night he dreamt of soft beds, chocolate cake, his mother and father's smiling faces and even his little sister!

Billy went to see the captain. "Please, sir, I want to go home," he said.

"Shiver me timbers!" said the captain to all his bloodthirsty crew. "See here, me hearties, me cabin boy Billy wants to go home. Shall we show 'im the way?" And he laughed a deep belly-rumbling laugh.

The pirates guffawed and cackled. They pointed at Billy and laughed so hard that they fell over.

And then they started to prepare the gangplank.

The gangplank stuck out over the edge of the pirate ship with nothing but the big waves crashing down below. "Off you go then, Billy Boy," laughed the captain. "Down to Davy Jones' locker."

"Help!" thought Billy. "I wish I could swim."

He walked to the end of the plank. Well, he had to because the captain's dagger was in his back. Down he tumbled into the crashing waves and joined the fish in the cold wet sea. Splash!

Billy didn't notice the fish because his mouth was so full of salty seawater. He wondered what Davy Jones' locker was and hoped there was something nice in it. He began to feel rather worried when the salty seawater stopped him from breathing, because he knew that you need to go on breathing if you want to go on living.

Now, fortunately, some beautiful mermaids happened to be playing with the fish at that very moment. Mermaids love teasing pirates and they felt sorry for Billy, so they pulled him up to the surface and showed him how to kick his legs and move his arms to keep himself afloat. A passing turtle joined in the

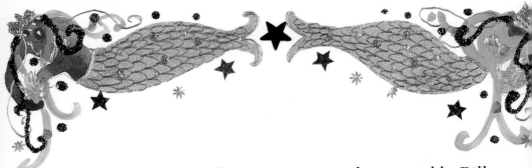

swimming lesson and it was amazing how quickly Billy learned with encouraging words and kind faces instead of shouts and scowls. In no time at all, they had swum all the way home. Billy thanked his new friends and waved goodbye.

His mother and father were so happy to see him. There was chocolate cake for tea, and his baby sister gave him a wet kiss. He told them all about his adventures and promised never to run away again.

His mum said, "I don't like the sound of that captain."

His dad said, "I do like the sound of those mermaids!"

His baby sister didn't say much but she liked hearing about the fish and the turtle and blew bubbles.

At bedtime, when he was warm and cosy, Billy said, "Mum, I've been thinking, could I please have mermaids on my duvet cover instead of pirates? Oh, and Mum, it's great to be back – there's no place like home!"